We're on an adventure!
What will we find?

We're hunting for treasure
of the wild kind!

We'll follow the trail
to see where it goes.

Where will it take us?
Nobody knows!

Look at these sticks
from this knobbly old tree!

We could be pirates,
on a ship out at sea!

Or wizards with wands
in a magical wood.

Building a den —
now that would be good!

We'll paddle through puddles
and squelch through the mud.

Then climb over tree stumps
and hunt for some bugs!

Look what we've found –
so tiny in size!

We'd better not touch, though –
just watch with our eyes.

Let's quietly tiptoe,
so we can see

a little blue bird
singing high in a tree.

Look, it's a feather!
Let's see if it floats.

It bobs on the water,
just like a sailboat!

On with our journey!
What else will we find?

Look at these leaves —
there are so many kinds!

Sssh! Let's be still.
What's that strange sound?

Some rustling and rumbling?
What could we have found?

It's only Ben's tummy,
and we're hungry too!

Let's stop now and eat, Goose.
Here's something for you!

What brilliant discoveries
we've all made today.

We've had a great time
and we wish we could stay!

The day's almost over.
What wild fun we've had!

It's time to go home now.
Oh Goose, don't be sad!

With the riches we've found
there's lots we can do.

Lead the way home, Goose!
Let's make something for you!

We love the outdoors,
and to tumble and run.

But making friends happy
is just as much fun!

For everyone who loves an adventure!
I hope this story inspires many more,
no matter how big or small.

ISBN 978-1-78270-254-2

First published 2017

Published by Award Publications Limited,
The Old Riding School, Welbeck,
Worksop, S80 3LR

www.awardpublications.co.uk

17 2

Printed in Turkey

Also available:

Goose
Goose Goes to School
Goose Goes to the Zoo
Happy Birthday, Goose!
Goose on the Farm
Goose Goes Shopping
Goose at the Beach
Goose's Spooky Surprise